Midnight th

Learns about Cooperation

by Karen Putzke

illustrated by Lara Lombardo

ISBN 978-1-934666-17-3

Published and distributed by:
High-Pitched Hum Publishing
321 15th Street North
Jacksonville Beach, Florida 32250

Contact High-Pitched Hum Publishing at www.highpitchedhum.net

To my family. You are the loves of my life.
And to my first horse, Premier.
You are a special dream-come-true.

Midnight the Cow was a young cow who lived on Farmer Nelson's farm. Midnight the Cow was usually quite pretty. But, she was just about to become especially beautiful.

Farmer Nelson's niece, Janie, was giving Midnight a bath because she was taking her to the county fair the next morning. Midnight enjoyed the long bath with fruity smelling shampoo and warm water.

Janie made sure all the grass and mud stains were cleaned from Midnight's legs, neck, and stomach. She made sure that Midnight had a really clean muzzle and really clean ears. She even made sure that Midnight's tail was spotless.

"There, Midnight. You're all clean! You are so beautiful," said Janie in her sweet voice. Midnight was happy to hear those words. Midnight thought she could surely win a ribbon for Janie.
The judges always like to see cows with shiny coats and polished hooves.

"Oh, Midnight, pleeeeeease stay clean tonight," pleaded Janie. "We'll be leaving first thing in the morning." And after leading Midnight back to her stall in the barn and patting her on the head, Janie walked back to her uncle's home.

Midnight thought to herself, "I'll just eat my dinner, lie down in the clean straw, and go to sleep.
That way I'll stay clean."

Sheldon appeared from around the corner.
"Heeeeeeey, Midnight," Sheldon bleated softly.
"I noticed you were getting a bath. What's going on?"

"Oh, hello, Sheldon. Janie got me all cleaned up
because I'm going to the fair tomorrow morning. I
think the fair will be coooooool!" exclaimed Midnight.

"That's great news, Midnight! I'm going to go tell Laney! She'll be thrilled, too!" Sheldon turned to find Laney, the barnyard chicken. But as he trotted away, he knocked over a pail of grain and molasses that Janie had left for Midnight.

"Great," thought Midnight. "Now I have molasses all over my hoooooooves!"

A few minutes later, Sheldon returned with Laney.

Laney clucked, "You look great, Midnight! I heard you were going to the fair. How exciting!"

"Yes, I can't wait! But now I have a problem. I'm supposed to stay clean, but look at my hooooooves. They're all sticky with moooooolasses."

"Oh, that is a problem," replied Laney. She flew up and over Midnight; but as she did, mud dripped off her claws onto Midnight's back.

Now, Midnight had sticky hooves and a muddy back! She was so sad thinking about how Janie would be disappointed. Midnight started sobbing.

Just then, Premier the Wise Pony came by and asked, "What's all the commotion?"

Midnight answered sadly, "Just look at me."

Laney chimed in, "Midnight was supposed to stay clean because Janie is taking her to the county fair tomorrow. Sheldon and I accidentally got her dirty."

Premier thought and declared, "Hey! We can cooperate and clean her up!"

Midnight, Sheldon, and Laney asked, "What??"

"Cooperation," Premier explained, "is where we work together to get a job done. And our job is to get Midnight cleaned up again!"

They quickly decided who would do what.

Laney took a sponge off the shelf in the barn. She put it in her beak and wiped each of Midnight's hooves.

Sheldon picked up a towel and handed it to Premier. Premier cleaned Midnight's back, wiping off every speck of mud.

"Wow! I must look clean now," said Midnight. "I can get a good night's sleep and be ready for the fair in the morning. Thank you all for cooperating to help make me clean again. You were right, Premier. By cooperating, we can get a job done tooooogether!"

Her friends stayed in the barn with her.
Laney nestled next to Sheldon, who was nestled next
to Premier. Midnight decided she'd better lie down in
her own clean straw.

Morning came and Janie hurried out to the barn.
"Midnight! Are you ready to go, girl?"

She was happy to see that Midnight was clean and
ready for the fair. Janie never knew that all the
animals had worked so hard to get Midnight as clean
as she was after her bath!

The day of the fair was sunny. Everyone was busily showing their animals, riding rides and eating corndogs and cotton candy. Janie showed Midnight against some other very nice, clean cows. Would Midnight win a prize?

Yes! The judge awarded Midnight a blue ribbon.
Janie kissed Midnight as the ribbon was
placed around her neck.

Midnight knew that cooperating
with her friends was a good thing!

The end.

About the Author

Karen Putzke, M.Ed., is a wife, mother and educator of students with special needs. She loves animals, books, and kids! She wishes to thank God, her family for unending support and love, and many friends who cheer for Midnight, Karen, and Lara. Karen lives in Northeast Florida on a horse farm with her family, horses, dogs, cats, rabbit and guinea pig - but no cow.

About the Illustrator

Lara Lombardo is a high school student who has been drawing for most of her life. Her whimsical illustrations are perfect for children's books and she expresses her unique perspective through her artwork. Lara is grateful to Mrs. Putzke for recognizing her talents and giving her this opportunity to follow her dream of becoming a children's book illustrator.

Visit our website for questions about this story and for fun activities with Midnight and her friends.

www.midnightthecow.com